What is goodbye?

NIKKI GRIMES
Illustrations by RAÚL COLÓN

Hyperion Books for Children   New York

Text copyright © 2004 by Nikki Grimes
Illustrations copyright © 2004 by Raúl Colón

First Edition
1 3 5 7 9 10 8 6 4 2

Printed in Mexico

Reinforced binding

Library of Congress Cataloging-in-Publication Data
Grimes, Nikki.
What is goodbye? / Nikki Grimes; illustrated by Raúl Colón—1st ed.
p.   cm
Summary: Alternating poems by a brother and sister convey their feelings about
the death of their older brother and the impact it had on their family.
ISBN 0-7868-0778-4
1. Death—Juvenile poetry. 2. Grief—Juvenile poetry. 3. Children's poetry, American.
[1. Death—Poetry. 2. Grief—Poetry. 3. Brothers and sisters—Poetry.
4. American poetry.] I. Title.
PS3557.R489982 W46 2004
811'.54—dc21
2002072987

Visit www.hyperionchildrensbooks.com

For my teacher Evelyn Wexler,
who encouraged me to grab hold of life
in the face of my father's death.
—N.G.

In memory of John—you made us smile.
—R.C.

What is goodbye?
Where is the good in it?
One leaves
and many hearts
are broken.
There must be
a better arithmetic
somewhere.

Getting the News ~ Jesse

My ears aren't working.
My hearing's broke.
Mom's lips are moving.
Is this some joke?
Why can't I make out
a single word?
My sister's crying.
What has she heard?
Somebody tell me!
Why are you sad?
Something's happened.
Something bad.
Why can't I feel
my hands anymore?
The only thing
I know for sure
is that my mother
couldn't have said
my big brother,
Jaron, is dead.

Getting the News ~ Jerilyn

Daddy told me in a whisper
sharp as a switchblade
and just as sly.
Blood ran before I
felt the cut.
"Jaron won't be
coming home anymore,"
he said.
"What?"
Silent, he stepped away,
turned himself like
a page in a book
so I couldn't read,
couldn't look inside.
Mommy also hid,
her eyes dull coins
peeking from the pockets
of her lids.
No one would look at me.

Oh, God. Oh, God!
There must be
somewhere I can go
something I can do.
What's that shiver
on my spine?
Jaron?
Is it you?

Saturday is here at last.
Time for soccer! What a blast.
Sun is shining. Skies are clear.
Weatherman's been wrong all year.

Uniform's all cleaned and pressed.
Can't wait till I'm washed and dressed.
Jeri hits the shower first,
takes all day. Girls are the worst!

Once I'm in, splish, splash, I'm done.
Minutes later, I'm the one
pouring cereal and juice,
hair still dripping, laces loose.

In a hurry. Got to go.
Here comes Mommy, shuffling slow,
hair all wild. She needs a comb.
What did she say? Stay at home?

What did you do, Jesse? Think!
Leave a dirt ring in the sink?
Bedroom's clean. I swept the floor.
So, what am I grounded for?

"Do I have to mow the lawn?
It's not my turn. It's—" Oh. He's . . .
Seasick stomach. Run outside.
Grab my bike and ride, ride, ride....

Sleep would not pay me a visit.
It refused to excuse yesterday
as nightmare.
Looks like death is true as sunshine.
No time to think about it, though.
Too much to do.
I iron Daddy's shirt
crisp as lettuce,
fry up a breakfast
of potatoes and eggs, which
I spoon up for Mommy.
I ignore the salty tracks
on her cheek, grope blindly
for a dishcloth, and scour
the kitchen counter.
I dust. I sweep.
I learn each windowpane
by name.
I keep moving
so the hours will chase
each other to the end of a day
I could really
do without.

The Funeral ～ Jesse

They tell me I'm too young to go,
to stay at home. To wait alone.
But how am I supposed to know
my brother's really dead?

Suppose the whole thing's just a lie?
Suppose he left? Shipped out to sea?
Suppose he couldn't say goodbye
but simply disappeared?

They should have taken me along.
Instead, I lie across his bed
and sniff his shirt, his scent so strong,
he's *here*, inside my head.

The Funeral ~ Jerilyn

I'm not sure I want to be here,
but someone has to take care
of my mother, and father,
who aren't able anymore.
Their hurt is like a tunnel,
and all they can see
is the dark.
It's up to me
to keep them from bumping
into walls.
So while the preacher speaks
and the choir sheds a tear
in the key of C,
I hold Mommy's hand,
rub a circle of comfort
into Daddy's back,
and squint at the casket
from eyes like slits.

There, nestled among roses
no one wants to smell,
is Jaron—
not a him, but an *it*,
some fake container,
wearing clothes stolen
from my brother's closet.
But where is *he*?

I push down the scream
that rings in me.
Suddenly,
I need to believe
in Heaven.

The Awful After ~ Jesse

I hang around
the edges of the room,
watch strangers nibble
on fruit and cake,
like at the wake.

Folks talk about
how Jaron is "asleep,"
"at rest," "at peace."
My sister groans.
She's not alone.

Why won't they leave?
Why did they even come?
My sister holds me.
I break and run.
I need some fun.

The Awful After ~ Jerilyn

I bite my tongue bloody
from holding it what seems
like hours.
I wander through this
silly crowd, wondering why
no one tells the truth.
Dead is dead.
Not "gone away."
Not "lost."
Not "on a journey."
Not "passed"—as if
my brother's life
were some test
he got a good grade on,
and now he's gone.
No! Call it what it is:
His body's in a grave.
There is no journey
he'll be coming
back from.

Why? ~ Jesse

Why did Jaron have to die?
I asked till my lips burned dry.
Mommy sighed and shook her head.
"God scoops up the good," she said.
Then, from now on, I won't be.
Hear that, God? Don't come for me.

Why? ~ Jerilyn

Why give God
a bad name?
Why not blame
the moon,
if you must pretend
to have an answer?
We both know sense
is like shadow.
Chase it till you sweat,
and all you'll get
is a handful
of nothing.

Besides, what difference
does it make?
Just concentrate
on breathing.

Night Noise ~ Jesse

Something's keeping
me from sleeping.
I hear sniffles
through the wall.

"Daddy, is that
you?" I whisper,
hearing crying
'cross the hall.

Further down
in bed I burrow,
pillow clamped
over my ears.

I'll go crazy
if I listen
to my daddy's
private tears.

Night Noise ~ Jerilyn

My teeth chatter
in the winter
of dreams.
I lie in a coffin,
beyond the reach
of worry,
Jaron floating
over me.
Something deep inside
screams, "No!"
and I wake to the sound
of my own fear.
Two years are all
that separate Jaron and me.
Two years
and a coffin.
I can't help thinking
Death could happen
to me.
Growing up?
Growing old?
The way I figure, now
there's no guarantee.

First Fear ~ Jesse

Me and Lucky
two of a kind.
Boy and dog whimpering.
Does Jeri mind?

She sits by me,
red-eyed but strong.
Jeri says crying
is never wrong.

"Jeri?" I ask.
"Will Dad die, too?
And what about Mom?
And what about you?"

Her skinny arms
embrace me tight.
"We're not going anywhere,
Jess. All right?"

She seems so sure.
Sis never lies.
I lean on her
and close my eyes.

First Fear ~ Jerilyn

Look at him,
head buried
in the black cushion
of Lucky's coat,
tears raw as rain.
How can I tell him
I'm afraid?
I say, "It's okay, Jess.
I'm sad, too,"
then wrap my sadness
around us both
like a blanket
and let him curl up
in the quiet.
I don't tell him
I'm worried about Mom.
I don't tell him
my friend's mom
lost her baby
then lost her mind.
Why multiply his fears?
They're better divided
between us.

First Day Back ~ Jesse

One stupid word
echoes through my day:
sorry. Sorry. SORRY.
I hate that word!
I punch the air
and storm away.

First Day Back ∽ Jerilyn

No one to mother, here.
I drop my guard too soon,
forget there are tears
waiting in the wings.
They show up on the scene
in the middle of P.E., but
I catch them quick,
shove them back in place.
"You're not doing this to me,"
I tell them.
        I'm the strong one.
        I'm in charge.

Catching a Glimpse ∼ Jesse

Yesterday, I saw him
playing basketball.
I yelled from the school bus.
Did he hear me call?

Jimmy laughed and spit out,
"That boy's in the dirt!"
"Take that back!" I screamed, then
punched him till I hurt.

I spent that whole morning
with the principal.
So what? That kid knew I'd
had a bellyful!

Catching a Glimpse ～ Jerilyn

I look for him, everywhere.
Not like Jesse, expecting
to find him around
the next corner,
but I look for traces.
In Mommy's eyes,
Daddy's grin,
the thick lashes he and Jesse
shared like twins.
I say these things to my parents,
but they don't want to know.
"Let's not talk about
him anymore, Jeri.
Please," they beg.
Then Mommy cries,
so I get the point.
I'm all alone in this.
"Okay," I say,
learning to lie better
day after day.

His Name ∾ Jesse

Mommy won't say Jaron's name
so I write it everywhere,
on the walls, my book, his chair.
If I'm punished, I don't care.
Let her take away my pens.
I'll write it on the air!

His Name ～ Jerilyn

Once, I asked my mother
where she found
Jaron's name.
In Hebrew
his name means "to sing,"
which he did
in every room
of this house.
His bass,
sweet as chocolate,
melted through the walls
at all hours of the day
and night.
I might not miss him
half as much
if his silence
didn't ring
so loudly.

Home Run ~ Jesse

I was last at bat today.
Our team held two bases.
Pow! I knocked one out of the park.
You should have seen their faces!

I took off around the field,
legs pumping like lightning!
I slid into home plate clean.
Man, I'm so cool, I'm frightening!

There you go, frowning again.
What's the matter, Mommy?
Nowadays, when I have fun,
you lay guilt trips on me.

What am I supposed to do,
spend each minute crying?
I wish I could please you, Mom,
but I'm sick of trying.

Home Run ~ Jerilyn

Jesse's eyes flash
a hint of sparkle
not seen since Christmas.
It's his right to smile,
isn't it?
To be delirious?
So what if I don't understand?
This ghost town,
draped in shadow,
is desperate for
a few more watts of light.
A crooked smile, warm as toast,
just might do us all
some good.
Lord knows, these walls
are splattered with
more than enough tears
to go around.
Even the dog is lonely
for the sound
of laughter.

Regrets ~ Jesse

I sneer into the mirror
raging at the traitor standing there.
How could he go all day
without thinking of his brother?
Doesn't he even care?

Regrets ~ Jerilyn

I yelled at him
that morning,
don't ask me why.
My so-called reason
is small enough
to dance on the head
of a pin.
What if
my hate-filled eyes
flashed before him
at the end?
What if
I say I'm sorry?
What if
he says, "Too late"?

Dinner ~ Jesse

We sit in our old places
with fake smiles on our faces,
ignoring his empty chair.

I tell some jokes like he did,
but Jeri says they're stupid.
Guess I don't have his flair.

Why did I even try it?
I sink in the lonely quiet
and wonder why life isn't fair.

Dinner ∼ Jerilyn

Dinner used to be
a noisy business
of Mom mining
for information
about everyone's day
and Jesse interrupting
and Lucky barking for
Jaron to drop a few
tasty scraps on the floor
accidentally on purpose
and Jaron trying to cover
by telling a joke so lame
I had to laugh
till Dad called us
to order.
Dinner is noiseless now
except for the clink
of knife and fork,
or functional chatter
like "Pass the butter, please."
As for Dad, he's
got enough order
to last a lifetime.

Lately ∼ Jesse

Lately, fights find me
everywhere I go.
Jeri says that I find *them*.
Maybe. I don't know.

I know I miss Jaron
more than I can stand.
I guess I ball up the hurt
and pound it with my hand.

Last week, my teacher
brought me a sketch pad.
"Draw in this," he told me,
"next time you feel mad."

First, I thought, *He's crazy!*
Now, I'm not so sure.
Though I'm mad as ever,
I don't fight anymore.

Lately ～ Jerilyn

Lately,
Daddy's been watching me
like I'm some egg on boil,
wondering if
there's still water
in the pot;
wondering if
my shell's about to crack;
wondering when
I'll burst.
What does he want from me?
I'm doing the best I can.
Why won't he let me be?

Places ~ Jesse

I don't like the barber's—
which my brother knew.
Sometimes he pretended
to hate barbers, too.

"Let's go do our man thing,"
my brother would say.
And we'd catch a bus to
the barber's that day.

We'd talk while we waited.
We'd play-fight and grin.
Sometimes we'd arm wrestle
and he'd let me win.

Then we'd get our hair clipped.
I'd get mine like his....

        I'm not going back there,
        and that's all there is.

Places ∽ Jerilyn

The last time he said it,
I was standing right here,
golden in the glory
of my grown-up ways,
talking boys,
hands on hips,
comparing lip gloss
with best friends
while we waited
for the bus.
Then here he comes,
calling me "Linnie,"
his little-girl name for me
since I was three,
the one he used
just to make me mad.
Once in a while, though
he'd use it in a sweet,
singsongy way
as if to say,
"I'm still your big brother,
the one you can come to,
the one who loved you
when you were toothless."

Rush ~ Jesse

Buck up! Be brave!
Get over it!
Those words make me
just want to spit.

Folks wind my sadness
like a clock.
"Time's up," they say.
Tick tock, tick tock.

"Forget your tears.
You've cried enough.
You've lost someone.
We know that's tough,

but now it's time
to move along."
They're telling me
my heart is wrong

for hurting past
the date they set?
Well, I'm not ready
to move on yet.

Rush ∼ Jerilyn

I come home from school,
find traces of my mother
everywhere—
Floors vacuumed,
clean clothes folded
and perched
on the edge of my bed,
Crock-Pot bubbling
in the kitchen.
Traces of mother.
But no *her*.
She hides in the dungeon
of her room,
silence the only key
that lets me in.
Last night, though,
she came down to watch TV
and I eased myself
on the sofa beside her,
dreamed we were
holding hands
the way we used to.
How long has it been?

I hold the question in,
like a deep breath,
till I turn blue. *Mommy,*
When will you look up?
When will you see
you've still got Jesse and me?
Please hurry.
We're lonely here
without you.

Mad ∼ Jesse

You promised I could
always count on you.
You swore you'd teach me
everything you knew.

When I got older,
we were going to bike
across the country.
We were going to hike

through Yellowstone then
through Yosemite.
How could you die and
break your word to me?

You're nothing but a
lying little rat.
You left me, Jaron.
I hate you for that!

Mad ~ Jerilyn

"I WISH YOU
WERE NEVER BORN!"
I scream,
bruising my lungs,
surprised there is air enough
left to breathe.
And why bother?
With every step I take
I slice my feet
on the jagged pieces
you've smashed
our family into.
But you're a ghost,
so what do you care?
Death has satisfied
your appetite
for attention.
You should be
happy now, Jaron.
Just don't expect me
to forgive you.

Out of Nowhere ~ Jesse

It almost feels like any other day.
I'll do my homework, go outside to play.
Who knows? Maybe I'll watch TV,
or— Hey! What's that truck passing me?
Salvation Army. Who called— No!
God, please tell me it's not so!
Mommy wouldn't toss his stuff.
Would she? Man, I've had enough!

Out of Nowhere ～ Jerilyn

I enter Jaron's room to dust
like the maid he turned me into
whenever I lost a bet.
The memory makes me smile
until I notice his closet,
naked as morning,
not a single shirt waving
from the railings.
I yank his dresser drawers,
find them empty, weightless
as rag dolls,
and fly from the room,
fire in my eyes.
One look burns my mother
to the ground.
"What have you done?
You had no right!"
She is stunned.
"What?" I spit.
"You think I have no feelings
because I never cry?"

And then I do,
great wrenching sobs
that split my chest
until I'm rescued
by exhaustion.

Down the Drain ～ **Jesse**

I draw a sailboat.
Jaron steers.
I wave from shore.
I draw in tears.

I draw him sailing
farther out,
too far to hear me
scream or shout.

I draw him smiling
"It's okay."
I draw us meeting
again someday.

The fist inside me
opens wide,
and out falls all
the hurt inside.

I keep on drawing
out my pain
until the worst
flows down the drain.

Down the Drain ∽ Jerilyn

I stumble across my journal,
forgotten among schoolbooks,
papers, and
my brother's obituary.
There you are, I think,
as if my journal is some
long-lost relative.
Then I realize
I'm the one
who's been gone.
They don't even have a name
for the country
I've been in
since Jaron died.
I haven't tried to write
for months. Now,
I flip to a page
blank as tomorrow,
and scribble in
that awful date.
This was the night,
I write,
that changed the world.

The Visit ~ Jesse

I hadn't seen
my cousins in a while.
There's something else
I hadn't seen for months:
My mother's smile.

Today, I got
two for one.

The Visit ~ Jerilyn

Uncle's visit brings out
the old family albums,
disturbing the dust
of weeks, and months, and
in the front are fading photos
of Daddy's family,
one big brood,
grinning gap-toothed
for the camera.
I count the children,
find one too many aunts.
Uncle explains how
one sister died when he was t
Daddy turtles into himself,
says it hurts too much
to talk about.
So I don't ask questions,
but file this much away:
He and Uncle are still here,
old as oaks.
Maybe I'll be around for
a few more years
after all.

Painless ∽ Jesse

My best friend's brother
picked him up from school.
He caught Sam in a headlock,
but the two of them were cool.
Sam's brother tickled him
like Jaron tickled me.
I couldn't help thinking
that's how it ought to be.
Inside, though, I was smiling
and all I felt was glad
that Sam and his brother share
what Jaron and I had.

Painless ≈ Jerilyn

Lost in lunchroom chatter
simple as sunrise,
the most serious matter
I face
is how much time
to spend with my friend
at the mall.
When should we meet?
Before homework?
After dinner?
We make plain plans,
which I can handle.
For now, we munch,
spill milk, and giggle over
little losses
like my loose-leaf,
stuffed with secret love notes.
It's missing,
and might become
a bothersome thing.
But life hums along,
and I feel no sting.

Connection ~ Jesse

I'm in my room the other day,
flipping baseball cards the way
Jaron showed me. I was eight.
Remembering is sometimes great.

Next thing I know, Dad's at my door.
He's been here maybe twice before.
He sits and asks me, "What's up, Jess?"
Ignores the fact my room's a mess.

"There's nothing much up, Dad," I say,
wondering why he's here today,
close enough to breathe my air.
But will he touch me? Will he dare?

Suddenly, he hugs me hard,
tugs my long hair, eyes my cards,
says, "We'll see a game this spring."
For now, like Jaron used to say,
        "Let's go do our man thing."

Connection ~ Jerilyn

This morning
I was draped
in Sunday sadness
heavy as the preacher's robe.
We sat in our usual pew,
the half-moon of Dad's eyes
trained on the altar,
like always.
Mom's hands
busy as tambourines,
kept the choir on the beat.
Jesse squirmed in his seat,
and Jaron—was missing,
making the scene familiar,
but not. Will anything ever
be the same?
It's more than Jaron
I'm missing.
It's the smile
Mom and I would share
whenever the choir hit
a sweet note,

and how she'd interrupt
her clapping long enough
to reach for my hand
and squeeze her love into it
the way—*Oh, yes!*
The way she did today.

Anniversary ~ Jesse

It's been a year.
What can I do
to mark the date?
Death's not a thing
to celebrate,
but something special
should be done.
I burn my drawings
one by one,
take the ashes
to his grave,
and say goodbye
at last,
and wave.

Anniversary ~ Jerilyn

Dear Jaron,
Wish you were here
above this mound.
I long for the sound
of shrill music
blasting from your room,
peeling my ear like
an apple.
Come back!
Play it again
and I'll sing along,
though
I only know the words
"I'll miss you forever."
P.S.
I'll leave this letter
in case you'd like to read it
once I'm gone.

Memories ~ Jesse

He taught me how to Rollerblade.
That first time I was so afraid

of flying out into the street.
I couldn't stop or steer my feet.

He could have laughed, you understand.
Instead, he simply took my hand

and showed me how to stop, and glide,
and turn. He never left my side.

Now every time I Rollerblade,
he lives in the memory we both made.

Memories ～ Jerilyn

On the day I turned six
my school friends descended
on our house for strawberry
ice-cream cake,
and pin the tail,
and music I can't remember
playing in the background.
My big brother
was too cool
to hang out with us
little kids,
but he did
because I asked him to.
He only stayed for a while,
but he danced me
round the room
for all to see.
We were something,
weren't we?

Ordinary Days ∼ Jesse

Mommy hums,
fussing over breakfast
like she's done
a thousand times before.

I count out
place mats, set the table,
desperate for
waffles. And nothing more.

Ordinary Days ~ Jerilyn

Seasons meander by
while pain melts into
memory.
An afternoon of soccer,
soda, and laughing
at silly jokes with friends
is no longer tinged
with guilt.
Ordinary days
are golden,
like ancient coins
recovered from
a treasure hunt.
More of them is
what I want
now that I've learned
to spend
or save each one
as if
it matters.

Photograph ∼ Poem for Two Voices

Jesse

It's time

for a new photograph.

Say "cheese."

Hold that pose!
Wait till you see it,
Mom and Dad,

a new kind of family.

One piece

we're whole again.
Whole again.

Smile!

Jerilyn

It's time
for a new photograph.
Squeeze in close.

Don't laugh.
Hold that pose!
Wait till you see it,

Jesse and me,
a new kind of family.
One piece.

One piece missing, but
we're whole again.

Whole again!
Smile!

∾ Author's Note ∾

There is no right or wrong way to feel when someone close to you dies. I found that out at fifteen when my father died. Some people cry right away, others don't. Some get angry, others don't. Some can talk about the person, while others find it impossible. Almost everyone asks why, but no one really has the answer. All we know for certain is that when someone we love dies, it hurts.

The way you feel is the way you feel. You have nothing to apologize for. What matters most is finding a healthy way to get your feelings out. I hope this book helps you do that.

—N.G.

~ Acknowledgments ~

I owe a debt of gratitude to Dr. Maribeth Ekey, who helped me find psychologists specializing in grief counseling for children. Thanks go to Carol Rhodes and Rosemary R. Chiaferi of Los Angeles, California, and Lila Delke of Spokane, Washington, who took time away from their busy practices to be interviewed for this book. Their expertise served as a guide for me in the writing of this collection.

I'm especially grateful to Earl A. Grollman for his landmark work, *Talking About Death: A Dialogue between Parent and Child*. His work helped me to shape my inspiration.

Thanks to psychologist Donna Mason-Blasi, who was kind enough to read the manuscript in its early stages.

Last but not least, special thanks to my agent, Elizabeth Harding, for her substantial support on this project. Her name belongs on this list of people who helped me realize my vision for this work.